"RIVETING!"—Rex Reed

"TAUT, ELOQUENT...HIS SCENES BRISTLE WITH CONFLICT."—*Women's Wear Daily*

AGNES of GOD

JOHN PIELMEIER began his career acting at many regional theaters, among them the Actors Theatre of Louisville, where *Agnes of God* had its premiere in March 1980. It had a seventeen-month run on Broadway, and was included in the *Burns Mantle Best Plays of 1981–82*. Mr. Pielmeier's other plays include *Haunted Lives*, a collection of one-act plays published by Dramatists Play Service; *Courage*, a one-man show about J. M. Barrie, which premiered in Louisville and subsequently opened in the new theater at the Lambs' Club in New York City; *Sleight of Hand* and *The Boys of Winter*, both of which will be produced in New York during the 1985–86 season; and *Jass*, which was presented at the 1985 O'Neill Conference. Mr. Pielmeier wrote the screenplay for the film version of *Agnes of God*, and is a past recipient of both an NEA grant and a Shubert Fellowship.

AGNES
of GOD

by john pielmeier

With a Special Introduction
by the Author

A PLUME BOOK

NEW AMERICAN LIBRARY

NEW YORK AND SCARBOROUGH, ONTARIO

To The Lady

INTRODUCTION

I started writing *Agnes* in February of 1978, but as with all my literary forays, the impetus to write began months before. For some time I had become increasingly concerned with questions of my Catholic heritage and the historical context of some of its issues. The questions I asked myself—are there saints today? miracles? did these phenomena ever exist and, if so, have they or our perception of them changed?—paralleled, I feared, some kind of personal religious awakening. I had always been spiritually concerned, but for some years had been a member of that set of disenchanteds called lapsed Catholics. The journey I was beginning was to become the very backbone of the play I determined to write.

It seemed to me arrogant and ultimately limiting, in examining my questions, to assume that the world as we know it (including any "immutable" laws of science) was exactly as it had been two thousand years ago. This observation only served to complicate matters for me, and it effectively blocked any answers. Then I realized that the asking of the questions was answer enough: that our determined search for *any* solution today has eliminated from our lives the mystery and wonder of the universe around us. And by any solution, I included theism as well as its opposite, and any nebulous fear of commitment that fell in between.

I now needed a dramatic platform on which to ask and explore my questions. One night, while drifting off to sleep, I remembered that some months before I had seen a headline in a daily scandal sheet. The headline read: "Nun Kills Baby." Now I wasn't interested in recreating this incident on the stage—I did no research into the actual event—but this plot seemed to create for me the perfect arena in which to attack and defend my thesis.

I wrote the play in no particular order (the Doctor's speech about trying to stop smoking was the first piece written), concentrating mostly on climactic scenes and then, in the summer of '78, with some spare time on my unemployed hands, filling in the rest. I had set aside a month to do some writing at my parents' home in Pennsylvania, my main task being the completion of a thriller begun some six months before. My mornings were filled with this work, but in the afternoons, simply to get my mind off the other play, I tackled *Agnes*. I completed it, and the thriller, in four weeks' time.

I had a cold reading of the new play at my apartment in September, my living room packed with encouraging friends. There are two comments from that evening that I remember: the play should be a two-acter (it was then a long one act), and the title should be changed. I listened to one, ignored the other, and rewrote. At a second reading in November the response was more positive. I rewrote again, sent the play to the Eugene O'Neill Playwrights' Conference—a wonderful summer gathering of professionals dedicated to the development of new scripts—and on May 1, 1979, received the news of acceptance.

I did three more sets of rewrites—one before the O'Neill Conference, one during, and one final after the conference was over. It was at this time that I added the "virgin birth" scene, one toward which I felt the play had been heading all along, and one which terrified me. I did not want anyone to think that this was *my* particular point-of-view—I found the premise pretty fantastic and about two inches away from being downright silly—but I thought at the same time it could be exciting, dangerous, and theatrical. The resulting Act Two confrontation is the most difficult scene for the actresses to play, yet serves as the play's very vulnerable center. It allows, I believe, those critics of the piece to write it off as pseudo-metaphysical nonsense, but it gives the evening its emotional heart and magic. I do not know, were I to write the play today, if the scene would appear in quite the same form, but it certainly represents the whole cloth of my writing experience in 1979, and for that reason is true to the spirit of *Agnes'* birth.

In September I was contacted by Actors' Theatre of Louisville, informing me that they wished to present *Agnes* in their Great American Play Festival in March. I asked for another staged reading, to which they consented—this one with a refreshing ten-day rehearsal period instead of the usual two to three days. I rewrote again, before and after the reading, and finally *Agnes* received its professional premiere on March 7, 1980. (In one preview night moment which could have been lifted from Mel Brooks' *The Producers*, the director and I, dismal with the slow pace of the evening's run, tiptoed into the theatre's bar, hid behind a pillar, and to our surprise listened to the audience's raves.)

In the theatre season of 1980-1981, *Agnes* received seven regional productions, one of which was at Baltimore's Center Stage. There it was seen by Lou Kramer, and then by Ken Waissman, the producers who would bring it to Broadway. A year and a half later, we were cast and ready to go.

This final rehearsal period was relatively free from rewrites. Once again I tackled the "virgin birth" scene, bringing in revision after revision, only to circle back to the original scene pre-tampering. Not that I believed these revisions were useless, for they served to strengthen the scene in my mind, and helped to lead the actresses, the director, and myself to the deeply felt through-line that makes the scene work. But the section of the play that caused me most problems was the doctor's final speech. It changed nightly and not until five days prior to the New York opening did it find its final form. Even now I waffle back and forth about its content, but have come to believe that at this point in the play it should not matter *what* is said but *how*: if the production is effective, the doctor could recite the local yellow pages and the audience, along with her, should be moved.

The play opened on March 30, 1982 at the Music Box Theatre and ran for seventeen months. By the time it closed, the film rights were still unsold.

This, I believe, is because the play was performed on

virtually an empty stage with no props and three actresses, which is about as deep into bare-bone theatre as you can get. Hollywood employs its share of unimaginative people and these I suppose did not think twice about *Agnes'* filmdom possibilities—there were none. But Norman Jewison, whom I first met at *Agnes'* somewhat disastrous Boston premiere and who was a supporter and believer all along, ignored everyone else and decided with his partner Patrick Palmer to produce the picture. I met with him over two December afternoons to talk about the adaptation, and our first and most important problem became location.

It was Norman's suggestion to set the film in Montreal. He is a native Canadian and this afforded him an opportunity to make a feature there, and of course production costs would be lower, but the most important reason for the decision was the strange combination of European and American atmosphere that French Canada could give us. Quebec is still a very Catholic province—crucifixes hang over the justices' courtroom benches—but its Catholicism, like the nuns in *Agnes*, is caught in the gears of progress. The province is filled with convents and monasteries built in the nineteenth century to house hundreds of nuns and monks which now either hold only a handful or, long since abandoned, none at all. There is a feeling of stopped time in these places, a sense of medieval isolation in the middle of the French-speaking America that I felt was ideal for telling sister Agnes's story.

Other problems were more obviously solved. Most of the psychiatrist's scenes were moved from her office to the convent, providing many more interesting visuals and locations. I had to tackle the question of Agnes' conception in greater detail, but this allowed me to reintroduce the importance of Sister Paul, an element I had dropped from the play, and to emphasize the psychiatrist-as-detective aspects of the film. All of the doctor's monologues had to be cut and their important facts somehow incorporated into the story, though it was often difficult to determine just what was important and what was pitchable. The Doctor had to be given a life outside the case—a mother, a boyfriend, other patients—but ultimately many of these scenes were eliminated. And finally, there was once again the problem of the final monologue, or in this case the final scene. It needed to walk a fine line between the inconclusive and the obvious, and the film needed to end on some uplifting note. (In one draft, Agnes threw herself off the bell tower: a pretty dismal uplift.) Since the story's conflict lies between Doctor Livingstone and Mother Miriam, I felt the final scene should be between the two of them—a very subtle all-is-forgiven scene. Several versions were written and shot, and as of this date I do not know which will be used in the final release. But then again, writing is twenty percent technique, thirty percent blood, and fifty percent guesswork.

And so, seven years after it was begun, my involvement with *Agnes* ends. She started out in the bassinet and is now graduating from college, and I must happily tend to the other infants in the nursery. Her journey is one taken by three women, taken (I hope) by an audience, taken by a playwright, taken by the play itself. And like all important journeys, it is a difficult one, an unsettling one, and hopefully a maturing one. And that, as someone once said, is miracle enough.

—John Pielmeier
May, 1985

ACKNOWLEDGMENTS

This play is a tribute to all of the women who have crossed my/its path:

To the three women who told me stories and who taught me how to tell them too: my mother Louise Blackburn Pielmeier, my aunt Marie Pielmeier, and my other mother Eleanor Morse.

To all of the women who have blessed these roles with their considerable talent: Anne Pitoniak, Adale O'Brien, Mia Dillon, Jo Henderson, Jacqueline Brookes, Dianne Wiest, Elizabeth Franz, Lee Remick, Elizabeth Ashley, Geraldine Page, Amanda Plummer, Diahann Carroll, Carrie Fisher, Maryann Plunkett, Mercedes McCambridge, Susan Riskin, Valerie Harper, Rosemary Murphy, Lily Knight, Susan Strasberg, Peggy Cass, Lynn Chausow, Jane Fonda, Anne Bancroft, Meg Tilly, and countless others.

To my special friend and agent, Jeannine Edmunds.

To my loving and beloved wife Irene O'Brien, who taught me how courageous, determined, and beautiful womanhood can be.

Agnes of God was first presented in a staged reading at the 1979 Eugene O'Neill Playwrights Conference on July 26, 1979. It was directed by Robert Allan Ackerman, and the cast was as follows:

DOCTOR MARTHA LIVINGSTONE	*Jo Henderson*
MOTHER MIRIAM RUTH	*Jacqueline Brookes*
AGNES	*Dianne Wiest*

The first professional production of *Agnes of God* opened on March 7, 1980 at the Actors Theatre of Louisville, Jon Jory Producing Director. It was directed by Walton Jones, with sets and lights by Paul Owen, and costumes by Kurt Wilhelm. The cast was as follows:

DOCTOR MARTHA LIVINGSTONE	*Adale O'Brien*
MOTHER MIRIAM RUTH	*Anne Pitoniak*
AGNES	*Mia Dillon*

Agnes of God opened on Broadway at the Music Box Theatre on March 30, 1982. It was presented by Kenneth Waissman, Lou Kramer, and Paramount Theatre Productions, and directed by Michael Lindsay-Hogg, with sets by Eugene Lee, lighting by Roger Morgan, and costumes by Carrie Robbins. The cast was as follows:

DOCTOR MARTHA LIVINGSTONE	*Elizabeth Ashley*
MOTHER MIRIAM RUTH	*Geraldine Page*
AGNES	*Amanda Plummer*

" '. . . why do you worry? What good would it do you if I told you she is indeed a saint? I cannot make saints, nor can the Pope. We can only recognize saints when the plainest evidence shows them to be saintly. If you think her a saint, she is a saint to you. What more do you ask? That is what we call the reality of the soul; you are foolish to demand the agreement of the world as well. . . .'

" 'But it is the miracles that concern me. What you say takes no account of the miracles.'

" 'Oh, miracles! They happen everywhere. They are conditional. . . . Miracles are things that people cannot explain. . . Miracles depend much on time, and place, and what we know and do not know. . . . Life is too great a miracle for us to make so much fuss about petty little reversals of what we pompously assume to be the natural order. . . . Who is she? That is what you must discover . . . and you must find your answer in psychological truth, not in objective truth. . . . And while you are searching, get on with your own life and accept the possibility that it may be purchased at the price of hers and that this may be God's plan for you and her.' "

ROBERTSON DAVIES,
Fifth Business

THE CHARACTERS

DOCTOR MARTHA LIVINGSTONE (pronounced "Li-ving-stun")
MOTHER MIRIAM RUTH
AGNES

The play is best served, I believe, by a stage free of all props, furniture and set pieces. The scenes flow one into another, without pause. Characters appear and disappear, and may even be present onstage when not in a particular scene. Because it is a play of the mind, and miracles, it is a play of light and shadows.

All parentheses in the dialogue indicate lines that are cut off or overlapped before the parentheses begin.

Throughout the evening, the doctor is never without a cigarette, except in her monologues and one or two other moments indicated in the script, until the end of the first act, after which she never smokes again.

—JOHN PIELMEIER

ACT I

ACT I

Scene 1

(*Darkness. A beautiful soprano voice is heard singing.*)

AGNES: *Kyrie eleison. Kyrie eleison. Kyrie eleison.*
Christe eleison. Christe eleison.
Kyrie eleison.

(*The lights softly rise on Doctor Martha Livingstone*)

DOCTOR: I remember when I was a child I went to see Garbo's *Camille*, oh, at least five or six times. And each time I sincerely believed she would *not* die of consumption. I sat in the theater breathless with expectation and hope, and each time I was disappointed, and each time I promised to return, in search of a happy ending. Because I believed in the existence of an alternate last reel. Locked away in some forgotten vault in Hollywood, Greta Garbo survives consumption, oncoming trains, and firing squads. Every time. I still want to believe in alternate reels. I still want to believe that somewhere, somehow, there is a happy ending for *every* story. It all depends on how thoroughly you look for it. And how deeply you need it.
(*Silence*)
The baby was discovered in a wastepaper basket with the umbilical cord knotted around its neck. The mother was found unconscious by the door to her room, suffering from excessive loss of blood. She was indicted for manslaughter and

brought to trial. Her case was assigned to me, Doctor
Martha Livingstone, as court psychiatrist, to determine
whether she was legally sane. I wanted to help . . . (this
young woman, believe me.)

ACT I

Scene 2

MOTHER: Doctor Livingstone, I presume? (*Mother laughs at her own joke*) I'm Mother Miriam Ruth, in charge of the convent where Sister Agnes is living.

DOCTOR: How do you do.

MOTHER: You needn't call me Mother, if you don't wish.

DOCTOR: Thank you.

MOTHER: Most people find it uncomfortable.

DOCTOR: Well . . .

MOTHER: I'm afraid the word brings up the most unpleasant connotations in this day and age . . .

DOCTOR: Yes.

MOTHER: . . . or it forces a familiarity that most are not willing to accept, right off the bat.

DOCTOR: I see.

MOTHER: So you may call me Sister. I've brought Sister Agnes for her appointment. They're allowing her to stay at the convent until the trial.

DOCTOR: Yes, I . . . (know.)

MOTHER: And I wanted to offer my help.

DOCTOR: Well, thank you, Sister, but I haven't even met Sister Agnes yet. If there's anything unclear *after* I speak to her, I'd . . . (be happy to talk to you.)

MOTHER: You must have tons of questions.

DOCTOR: I do, but I'd like to ask them of Agnes.

MOTHER: She can't help you there.

DOCTOR: What do you mean?

MOTHER: She's blocked it out, forgotten it. I'm the only one who can answer those questions.

DOCTOR: How well do you know her?

MOTHER: Oh, I know Sister Agnes very well. You see, we're a contemplative order, not a teaching one. Our ranks are quite small. I was chosen to be Mother Superior about four years ago, just prior to her coming to us. So I think I'm more than qualified to answer any questions you might have. Would you mind not smoking?

DOCTOR: Yes, I'm sorry, I should have asked if it bothered you. (*The doctor does not put out the cigarette, but waves the smoke in another direction*)

MOTHER: Never offer an alcoholic a drink, isn't that what they say?

DOCTOR: You were a smoker?

MOTHER: Two packs a day.

DOCTOR: Oh, I can beat that, Sister.

MOTHER: Lucky Strikes. (*The doctor laughs*) My sister used to say that one of the few things to believe in in this crazy world is the honesty of unfiltered cigarette smokers.

DOCTOR: You have a smart sister.

MOTHER: And you have questions. Fire away.

(*Silence*)

DOCTOR: Who knew about Agnes' pregnancy?

MOTHER: No one.

DOCTOR: How did she hide it from the other nuns?

MOTHER: She undressed alone, she bathed alone.

DOCTOR: Is that normal?

MOTHER: Yes.

DOCTOR: How did she hide it during the day?

MOTHER: (*Shaking her habit*) She could have hidden a machine gun in here if she wanted.

DOCTOR: And she had no physical examination during this time?

MOTHER: We're examined once a year. Her pregnancy fell in between our doctor's visits.

DOCTOR: Who found the baby?

MOTHER: I did. I'd given Sister Agnes permission to retire early that night. She wasn't feeling very well. I went to her room a short while later . . .

DOCTOR: The nuns have separate rooms?

MOTHER: Yes. And I found her unconscious by the door. I tried to revive her. When I couldn't I had one of the other sisters call for an ambulance. It was then that I found . . . the wastepaper basket.

DOCTOR: Found?

MOTHER: It was hidden. Against the wall, under the bed.

DOCTOR: Why did you think to look there?

MOTHER: I was cleaning. There was a lot of blood.

DOCTOR: Were you alone when you found it?

MOTHER: No. Another sister, Sister Margaret, was with me. It was she who called the police.

DOCTOR: Did you find a diary, letters?

MOTHER: I don't understand.

DOCTOR: Something to clue you in on the identity of the father.

MOTHER: Oh I see. No, I found nothing.

DOCTOR: Who could it have been?

MOTHER: I haven't a clue.

DOCTOR: What men had access to her?

MOTHER: None, as far as I know.

DOCTOR: Was there a doctor?

MOTHER: Yes.

DOCTOR: A man?

MOTHER: Yes, but I told you she never . . . (saw him.)

DOCTOR: Was there a priest?

MOTHER: Yes, but . . . (I don't see . . .)

DOCTOR: What's his name?

MOTHER: Father Marshall. But I don't see him as a candidate. He's very shy.

DOCTOR: Could there have been anyone else?

MOTHER: Obviously there was.

DOCTOR: Then why didn't you care to find out who?

MOTHER: Believe me, I cared very much at the time. I did everything short of asking Agnes, and still . . . (I have no idea how she got that child.)

DOCTOR: Why *didn't* you ask her?

MOTHER: If she doesn't even remember the birth, do you think she'd admit to the conception? Besides, I really don't see what this has to do with her.

DOCTOR: Oh, come on, Sister.

MOTHER: The *important* fact is that *somebody* gave her that baby, Doctor. That we know. But that happened some twelve months ago. I fail to see how the *identity* of that somebody has anything to do with the trial.

DOCTOR: Why do you think that?

MOTHER: Don't ask me those questions, dear. I'm not the patient.

DOCTOR: But *I'm* the doctor. *I'm* the one who decides what is or is not important here.

MOTHER: Yes.

DOCTOR: Then why are you avoiding my question?

MOTHER: I'm not . . . (avoiding.)

DOCTOR: Who was the father?

MOTHER: I don't know.

(*Silence*)

DOCTOR: I'd like to see her now.

MOTHER: Doctor, I don't know how to say this politely, but I don't approve of you. Not you personally, but—

DOCTOR: The science of psychiatry.

MOTHER: Yes. I want to ask you to deal with Agnes as speedily and as easily as possible. She's a fragile person. She won't hold up under *any* sort of cross-examination.

DOCTOR: Sister, I'm not with the Inquisition.

MOTHER: And I'm not from the Middle Ages. I know what you are. You're a surgeon. I don't want that mind cut open.

DOCTOR: Is there something in there you don't . . . (want me to see?)

MOTHER: I want you to be careful, that's all.

DOCTOR: And quick?

MOTHER: Yes.

DOCTOR: Why?

MOTHER: Because Agnes is different.

DOCTOR: From other nuns? Yes, I can see that.

MOTHER: From other people. She's special.

DOCTOR: In what way?

MOTHER: She's gifted. She's blessed.

DOCTOR: What do you mean? (*Agnes is heard singing*)

AGNES: *Gloria in excelsis Deo . . .*

MOTHER: There.

AGNES: *Et in terra pax hominibus bonae voluntatis.*

MOTHER: She has the voice of an angel.

AGNES: *Laudamus te.*
  Benedicimus te.

DOCTOR: Does she often sing when she's alone?

MOTHER: Always.

AGNES: *Adoramus te.*

MOTHER: She's embarrassed to sing in front of others.

AGNES: *Glorificamus te.*

DOCTOR: Who taught her?

MOTHER: I don't know.

AGNES: *Gratias agimus tibi propter magnam gloriam tuam.*
Domine Deus.
Rex coelestis.
Deus pater omnipotens.
Domini Fili unigenite
Jesu Christe.

MOTHER: (*During above*) When I first heard her sing, I was
thrilled. And I couldn't connect that voice with the simple,
happy child I knew. And she *was* happy, Doctor. But that
voice belongs to someone else.

AGNES: *Domine Deus,*
Agnus Dei,
Filius Patris,
Qui tollis peccata mundi,
Miserere nobis.

DOCTOR: Would you send her in, please?

MOTHER: You will be careful, won't you?

DOCTOR: I'm always careful, Sister.

MOTHER: May I stay?

DOCTOR: No. (*Mother smiles*)

MOTHER: I'll send her in.

ACT I

Scene 3

(Agnes continues to sing into this scene.)

AGNES: *Qui tollis peccata mundi*
Suscipe deprecationem nostram,
Qui sedes ad dexteram Patris,
Miserere nobis.
Quoniam tu solus sanctus,
Tu solus Dominus,
Tu solus Altissimus,
Jesu Christe.
Cum Sancto Spiritu
In gloria Dei Patris.

DOCTOR: *(Speaking over Agnes)* There was a lynching mob that came before a judge who accused them of hanging a man without a fair and objective trial. "Oh, your Honor," the leader said, "we listened *very* fairly and objectively to *every* word he had to say. Then we hung the son of a bitch."

I *wanted* to maintain my objectivity, but Mother Miriam wouldn't believe that. Oh, she couldn't have known about Marie but she must have suspected *something*. Marie was my younger sister, who decided she had a vocation to the convent when she was fifteen. So my mother sent her off without a second thought, and I never saw her again. I received a message late one night that Marie had died of

acute, and unattended, appendicitis because her Mother
Superior wouldn't send her to a hospital. (*She laughs*)
Well, no, I guess at heart I couldn't be very fair and objec-
tive, could I? But I tried.

(*Silence*)

I remember waiting to view Marie's body in a little convent
room, and staring at those spotless walls and floors and
thinking, my God, what a metaphor for their minds. And
that's when I realized that *my* religion, *my* Christ, is this.
The mind. Everything I do not understand in this world is
contained in these few cubic inches. Within this shell of
skin and bone and blood I have the secret to absolutely everything. I look at a tree and I think, isn't it wonderful that
I have created something so *green*. God isn't out there. He's
in here. God is you. Or rather you are God. Mother
Miriam couldn't understand that, of course. Oh, she reminded me so much of my own mother. And as for Agnes,
well . . . (just hearing her voice . . .) (*The doctor is in-
terrupted by Agnes' appearance*)

ACT I

Scene 4

AGNES: Hello.

DOCTOR: Hello. I'm Doctor Livingstone. I've been asked to talk to you. May I?

AGNES: Yes.

DOCTOR: You have a lovely voice.

AGNES: No I don't.

DOCTOR: I just heard you.

AGNES: That wasn't me.

DOCTOR: Was it my receptionist? You saw her, didn't you? The tall woman with the purple hair who looks like an ostrich?
(*Agnes smiles*)
That's not very nice to say, but she does, doesn't she?

AGNES: Yes.

DOCTOR: She wasn't singing now, was she? I remember one day she sang and broke a patient's eyeglasses.
(*Agnes laughs*)
You're very pretty, Agnes.

AGNES: No I'm not.

DOCTOR: Hasn't anyone ever told you that before?

AGNES: I don't know.

DOCTOR: Then I'm telling you now. You're very pretty. And you have a lovely voice.

AGNES: Let's talk about something else.

DOCTOR: What would you like to talk about?

AGNES: I don't know.

DOCTOR: Anything. First thing comes to your mind.

AGNES: God. But there's nothing to say about God.

DOCTOR: Second thing comes to your mind.

AGNES: Love.

DOCTOR: Why love?

AGNES: I don't know.

(*Silence*)

DOCTOR: Have *you* ever loved someone, Agnes?

AGNES: God.

DOCTOR: I mean have you ever loved another human?

AGNES: Oh, yes.

DOCTOR: Who is that?

AGNES: Everyone.

DOCTOR: Who in particular?

AGNES: Right now?

DOCTOR: Yes.

AGNES: I love you.

(*Silence*)

DOCTOR: But have you ever loved a man? Other than Jesus Christ.

AGNES: Yes.

DOCTOR: Who?

AGNES: Oh, there are so many.

DOCTOR: Well, do you love Father Marshall?

AGNES: Oh, yes.

DOCTOR: Do you think *he* loves *you?*

AGNES: Oh, I know he does.

DOCTOR: He told you that?

AGNES: No, but when I look into his eyes I can see.

DOCTOR: You've been alone together.

AGNES: Oh, yes.

DOCTOR: Often?

AGNES: At least once a week.

DOCTOR: (*Sharing Agnes' joy*) Did you like that?

AGNES: Oh, yes.

DOCTOR: Where do you meet?

AGNES: In the confessional.

(*A beat*)

DOCTOR: I see. Do you ever meet with him . . . (outside the confessional?)

AGNES: You want to talk about the baby, don't you?

DOCTOR: Would you like to talk about it?

AGNES: I never saw any baby. I think they made it up.

DOCTOR: Who?

AGNES: The police.

DOCTOR: Why should they?

AGNES: I don't know.

DOCTOR: Do you remember the night they said it came?

AGNES: No. I was sick.

DOCTOR: How were you sick?

AGNES: Something I ate.

DOCTOR: Did it hurt?

AGNES: Yes.

DOCTOR: Where?

AGNES: Down there.

DOCTOR: What did you do?

AGNES: I went to my room.

DOCTOR: What happened there?

AGNES: I got sicker.

DOCTOR: And then?

AGNES: I fell asleep.

DOCTOR: In the middle of all that pain?

AGNES: Yes.

DOCTOR: But where did the baby come from?

AGNES: What baby?

DOCTOR: The baby they made up.

AGNES: From their heads.

DOCTOR: Is that where they say it came from?

AGNES: No, they say it came from the wastepaper basket.

DOCTOR: Where did it come from before that?

AGNES: From God.

DOCTOR: *After* God, *before* the wastepaper basket.

AGNES: I don't understand.

DOCTOR: How are babies born?

AGNES: Don't you know?

DOCTOR: Yes, I think I do, but I want you to . . . (tell me.)

AGNES: I don't know what you're talking about! You want to talk about the baby, everybody wants to talk about the baby, but I never saw the baby, so I can't talk about the baby, because I don't believe in the baby!

DOCTOR: Then let's talk about something else.

AGNES: No! I'm tired of talking! I've been talking for weeks! And nobody believes me when I tell them anything! Nobody listens to *me!*

DOCTOR: I'll listen. That's my job.

AGNES: But I don't want to have to answer any more questions.

DOCTOR: Then how would you like to ask them?

AGNES: What do you mean?

DOCTOR: Just like that. You ask, I'll answer.

AGNES: Anything?

DOCTOR: Anything.

(*A beat*)

AGNES: What's your real name?

DOCTOR: Martha Louise Livingstone.

AGNES: Are you married?

DOCTOR: No.

AGNES: Would you like to be?

DOCTOR: Not at the moment, no.

AGNES: Do you have children?

DOCTOR: No.

AGNES: Would you like some?

DOCTOR: I can't have them anymore.

AGNES: Why?

DOCTOR: Well . . . I stopped menstruating.

AGNES: Why do you smoke?

DOCTOR: Does it bother you?

AGNES: No questions.

DOCTOR: Smoking is an obsession with me. I started smoking
when my mother died. She was an obsession, too. I suppose
I'll stop smoking when I become obsessed with something
else.
(*Silence*)
I bet you're sorry you asked. Any more questions?

AGNES: One.

DOCTOR: What's that?

AGNES: Where do *you* think babies come from?

DOCTOR: From their mothers and fathers, of course. Before that, I don't know.

AGNES: Well, I think they come from when an angel lights on their mother's chest and whispers into her ear. That makes good babies start to grow. Bad babies come from when a fallen angel squeezes in down there, and they grow and grow until they come out down there. I don't know where good babies come out.
(*Silence*)
And you can't tell the difference except that bad babies cry a lot and make their fathers go away and their mothers get very ill and die sometimes. Mummy wasn't very happy when *she* died and I think she went to hell because every-time I see her she looks like she just stepped out of a hot shower. And I'm never sure if it's her or the Lady who tells me things. They fight over me all the time. The Lady I saw when I was ten. I was lying on the grass looking at the sun and the sun became a cloud and the cloud became the Lady, and she told me she would talk to me and then her feet began to bleed and I saw there were holes in her hands and in her side and I tried to catch the blood as it fell from the sky but I couldn't see any more because my eyes hurt because there were big black spots in front of them. And she tells me things like—right now she's crying "Marie! Marie!" but I don't know what that means. And she uses me to sing. It's as if she's throwing a big hook through the air and it catches me under my ribs and tries to pull me up but I can't move because Mummy is holding my feet and all I can do is sing in her voice, it's the Lady's voice, God loves you!
(*Silence*)
God loves you.
(*Silence*)

DOCTOR: Do you know a Marie?

AGNES: No. Do you?

(*Silence*)

DOCTOR: Why should I?

AGNES: I don't know.

(*Silence*)

DOCTOR: Do you hear them often, (these voices?)

AGNES: I don't want to talk anymore, all right? I just want to go home.

ACT I

Scene 5

MOTHER: Well, what do you think? Is she totally bananas or merely slightly off center? Or maybe she's perfectly sane and just a very good liar. What have you decided?

DOCTOR: I haven't yet. What about you?

MOTHER: Me?

DOCTOR: Yes. You know her better than I do. What's your opinion?

MOTHER: Well . . . I believe that she's . . . *not* crazy. Nor is she lying.

DOCTOR: But how could she have a child and know nothing of sex and birth?

MOTHER: Because she's an innocent. She's a slate that hasn't been touched, except by God. There's no place for those facts in her mind.

DOCTOR: Oh, bullshit.

MOTHER: In her case it isn't. Her mother kept her home almost all of the time. She's had very little schooling. I don't know how her mother avoided the authorities but she did. When her mother died, Agnes came to us. She's never been "out there," Doctor. She's never seen a television show or a movie. She's never read a book.

DOCTOR: But if you believe she's so innocent, how could she murder a child?

MOTHER: She didn't. This is manslaughter, not murder. She did not consciously kill that baby. I don't know what *you'd* call it—whatever psychological-medical jargon you people use—but she was not conscious at the time. That's why she's innocent. She honestly doesn't remember. She'd lost a lot of blood, she'd passed out by the time I'd found her . . .

DOCTOR: You want me to believe that she killed that baby, hid the wastepaper basket, and crawled to the door, all in some sort of mystical trance?

MOTHER: I don't care *what* you believe. You're her psychiatrist, not her jury. You're not determining her guilt.

DOCTOR: Was there ever any question of that?

MOTHER: What do you mean?

DOCTOR: Could someone else have murdered that child?

(*Silence*)

MOTHER: Not in the eyes of the police.

DOCTOR: And in your eyes?

MOTHER: I've told you what I believe.

DOCTOR: That she was unconscious at the time, yes, so someone else could have easily come into her room and . . .
(done it.)

MOTHER: You don't honestly think . . . (something like that
happened.)

DOCTOR: It's *possible,* isn't it?

MOTHER: Who?

DOCTOR: I don't know, perhaps one of the other nuns. She
found out about the baby and wanted to avoid a scandal.

MOTHER: That's absurd.

DOCTOR: That possibility never occurred to you?

MOTHER: *No one* knew about Agnes' pregnancy. *No one.* Not
even Agnes.

(*Silence*)

DOCTOR: When did you first learn about this innocence of
hers, about the way she thinks?

MOTHER: A short while after she came to us.

DOCTOR: And you weren't shocked?

MOTHER: I was appalled. Just as you are now. You'll get used
to it.

DOCTOR: What happened?

MOTHER: She stopped eating. Completely.

DOCTOR: This was before her pregnancy?

MOTHER: Almost two years before.

DOCTOR: How long did this go on?

MOTHER: I don't know. I think it was about two weeks before it was reported to me.

DOCTOR: Why did she do this?

MOTHER: She refused to explain at first. She was brought before me—sounds like a tribunal, doesn't it?—and when we were alone she confessed.

DOCTOR: Well?

MOTHER: She said she'd been commanded by God.

(*Agnes appears. Throughout the scene, one of Agnes' hands is inconspicuously hidden in the folds of her habit*)

He spoke to you Himself?

AGNES: No.

MOTHER: Through someone else?

AGNES: Yes.

MOTHER: Who?

AGNES: I can't say.

MOTHER: Why?

AGNES: She'd punish me.

MOTHER: One of the sisters?

AGNES: No.

MOTHER: Who?

(*Silence*)

Why would she tell you to do this?

AGNES: I don't know.

MOTHER: Why do you think?

AGNES: Because I'm getting fat.

MOTHER: Oh, for Heaven's sake.

AGNES: I am. There's too much flesh on me.

MOTHER: Agnes . . .

AGNES: I'm a blimp.

MOTHER: . . . why does it matter whether you're fat or not?

AGNES: Because.

MOTHER: You needn't worry about being attractive here.

AGNES: I do. I have to be attractive to God.

MOTHER: He loves you as you are.

AGNES: No He doesn't. He hates fat people.

MOTHER: Who told you this?

AGNES: It's a sin to be fat.

MOTHER: Why?

AGNES: Look at all the statues. *They're* thin.

MOTHER: Agnes . . .

AGNES: That's because they're suffering. Suffering is beautiful. I want to be beautiful.

MOTHER: Who tells you these things?

AGNES: Christ said it in the Bible. He said, "Suffer the little children, for of such is the Kingdom of Heaven." I want to suffer like a little child.

MOTHER: That's not what . . . (He meant.)

AGNES: I *am* a little child, but my body keeps getting bigger. I don't want it to get bigger because then I won't be able to fit in. I won't be able to squeeze into Heaven.

MOTHER: Agnes, dear, Heaven is not . . . (a place with bars or windows.)

AGNES: (*Cupping her breasts*) I mean look at these. I've got to lose weight.

MOTHER: (*Reaching toward Agnes*) Oh my dear child.

AGNES: I'm too fat! Look at this—I'm a blimp! God blew up the *Hindenburg*. He'll blow up me. That's what she said.

MOTHER: Who?

AGNES: Mummy! I'll get bigger and bigger every day and then I'll pop! But if I stay little it won't happen!

MOTHER: Your mother tells you this?

(*Silence*)

Agnes, dear, your mother is dead.

AGNES: But she watches. She listens.

MOTHER: Nonsense. I'm your mother now, and I want you to eat.

AGNES: I'm not hungry.

MOTHER: You have to eat *something*, Agnes.

AGNES: No I don't. The host is enough.

MOTHER: My dear, I don't think a communion wafer has the Recommended Daily Allowance of *anything*.

AGNES: Of God.

MOTHER: Oh yes, of God.

AGNES: What does that word mean? Begod?

MOTHER: Bego*t*. You don't know?

AGNES: That God's my father?

MOTHER: Only spiritually. You don't know what that means? Begot?

AGNES: Bego*d*. That's what *she* calls it. But I don't understand it. She says it means when God presents us to our mothers, in bundles of eight pounds six ounces.

MOTHER: Oh my dear.

AGNES: I have to be eight pounds again, Mother.

MOTHER: You'd even drop the six ounces. Come here. (*Mother reaches out for an embrace. Agnes avoids the embrace, keeping the one hand concealed in her habit. Mother stares at the hidden hand*) Now what's wrong?

AGNES: I'm being punished.

MOTHER: For what?

AGNES: I don't know.

MOTHER: How? (*Agnes presents a hand wrapped in a bloody handkerchief*) What happened?

(*Agnes removes the handkerchief*)

Oh dear Jesus. Oh dear Jesus.

AGNES: It started this morning, and I can't get it to stop. Why me, Mother? Why me?

DOCTOR: How long did it last?

MOTHER: It was gone by the following morning.

DOCTOR: Did it ever come back?

MOTHER: Not that I know of, no.

DOCTOR: Why didn't you send her to a doctor?

MOTHER: I didn't see the need. She began eating again, and that's . . . (all that seemed important at the time.)

DOCTOR: You thought that's all there was to it? Get some food down her throat and she's all better?

MOTHER: Of course not. Look, I know what you're thinking. She's an hysteric, pure and simple.

DOCTOR: Not simple, no.

MOTHER: I *saw* it. Clean through the palm of her hand, do you think hysteria did that?

DOCTOR: It's been doing it for centuries—she's not unique, you know. She's just another victim.

MOTHER: Yes, God's victim. *That's* her innocence. She belongs to God.

DOCTOR: And I mean to take her away from Him—that's what you fear, isn't it?

MOTHER: You bet I do.

DOCTOR: Well, I prefer to look upon it as opening her mind.

MOTHER: To the world?

DOCTOR: To herself. So she can begin to heal.

MOTHER: But that's not your job, is it? You're here to diagnose, not to heal.

DOCTOR: That is a matter of opinion.

MOTHER: The judge's . . . (opinion.)

DOCTOR: *Your* opinion. I'm here to help her in whatever way I see fit. That's my duty as a doctor.

MOTHER: But not as an employee of the court. You're to make a decision on her sanity as quickly as possible and not interfere with due process of law. Those are the judge's words, not mine.

DOCTOR: As quickly as *I see fit,* not as possible. I haven't made
that decision yet.

MOTHER: But the kindest thing you can do for Agnes is to
make that decision and let her go.

DOCTOR: Back to court?

MOTHER: Yes.

DOCTOR: And what then? If I say she's crazy, she goes to an
institution. If I say she's sane, she goes to prison.

MOTHER: *Temporary* insanity, then.

DOCTOR: Oh yes. In all good conscience I can say that a child
who sees bleeding women at the age of ten, and eleven years
later strangles a baby is *temporarily* insane. No, Sister, this
case is a little more complicated than that.

MOTHER: But the longer you take to make a decision, the
more difficult it will be for Agnes.

DOCTOR: Why?

MOTHER: Because the world is a very damaging experience
for someone who hasn't seen it for twenty-one years.

DOCTOR: And you think the sooner she's in prison the better
off she'll be?

MOTHER: I'm hoping that whatever her sentence, the judge
will allow her to return to the convent and serve her time in
penance there.

(*Silence*)

DOCTOR: Well, we'll see about that.

MOTHER: You wouldn't allow her to return . . . (to the convent?)

DOCTOR: I wouldn't send her back to the source of her problem, no.

MOTHER: *Your* decision has nothing to do with where Agnes will serve . . . (her sentence.)

DOCTOR: My *recommendation* has *everything* to do with *everything*.

MOTHER: Then you'd send her to prison?

DOCTOR: Yes, if I felt she was guilty of a premeditated crime, I would.

MOTHER: Or an asylum?

DOCTOR: If I felt it would help her.

MOTHER: It would *kill* her.

DOCTOR: I doubt that.

MOTHER: I'm fighting for this woman's *life*, not her temporal innocence.

DOCTOR: Were you fighting for her life when you didn't even send her to a medical doctor?

MOTHER: What?

DOCTOR: She had a hole in the palm of her hand! She could have bled to death! And you wouldn't send her to a hospital! That child could have died, all because of some stupid . . . (irrational idea that she was better off at the convent.)

MOTHER: But she didn't die, did she?!

(*Silence*)

If anyone else had seen what I had seen, well, she'd be public
property. Newspapers, psychiatrists, ridicule. She doesn't
deserve that.

DOCTOR: But she has it now.

MOTHER: Yes. She does.

(*Agnes is heard singing. This continues into the next scene*)

AGNES: *Credo in unum Deum,*
   Patrem omnipotentem,
   factorem coeli et terrae
   visibilium omnium et invisibilium.
   Et in unum Dominum Jesum Christum,
   Filium Dei unigenitum.
   Et ex Patre natum
   ante omnia saecula.
   Deum de Deo,
   lumen de lumine,
   Deum verum de Deo vero.
   Genitum, non factum,
   consubstantialem Patri:
   per quem omnia facta sunt.
   Qui propter nos homines,
   et descendit de coelis.
   Et incarnatus est de Spiritu Sancto
   ex Maria Virgine:
   Et Homo Factus Est.

ACT I

Scene 6

(*Agnes' singing continues through the beginning of the scene.*)

DOCTOR: Oh, we would get into terrible arguments, my
mother and I. Once, when I was twelve or thirteen, I told
her that God was a moronic fairy tale—I think I'd spent an
entire night putting those words together—and she said,
"How dare you talk that way to me," as if *she* were the
slandered party. And shortly after Marie died, I became
engaged for a very short time to a very romantic French-
man whom my mother despised, and whom consequently I
adored. We screamed ourselves hoarse many a night over
that man.
(*She laughs*)
And you know, I haven't thought of him in years. I haven't
seen him since I left him—no, *pardonnez-moi*, Maurice,
since *he* left me. What finally happened was that I . . .
well, I . . . I was pregnant and I didn't exactly see myself
as a . . . well, as my mother. Maurice *did*, so . . .
(*Silence*)
And then once, in Mama's last years when she was not altogether lucid, I told her in a burst of anger that God was
dead, and do you know what she did? She got down on her
knees and prayed for His soul. God love her. I wish we
atheists had a set of words that meant as much as those
three do. Oh, I was never a devout Catholic—my doubts

about the faith began when I was six—but when Marie
died I walked away from religion as fast as my mind would
take me. Mama never forgave me. And I never forgave the
Church. But I learned to live with my anger, forget it even
. . . until *she* walked into my office, and every time I saw
her after that first lovely moment, I became more and more
. . . entranced.
(*Silence*)
Marie. Marie.

ACT I

Scene 7

AGNES: Yes, Doctor?

DOCTOR: Agnes, I want you to tell me how you feel about babies.

AGNES: Oh, I don't like them. They frighten me. I'm afraid I'll drop them. They're always growing, you know. I'm afraid they'll grow too fast and wriggle right out of my arms. They have a soft spot on their heads and if you drop them so they land on their heads they become stupid. That's where I was dropped. You see, I don't understand things.

DOCTOR: Like what?

AGNES: Numbers. I don't understand where they're all headed. You could spend your whole life counting and never reach the end.

DOCTOR: I don't understand them either. Do you think I was dropped on my head?

AGNES: Oh, I hope not. It's a terrible thing, one of the great tragedies of life, to be dropped on your head. And there are other things, not just numbers.

DOCTOR: What things?

AGNES: Everything, sometimes. I wake up and I just can't get hold of the world. It won't stand still.

DOCTOR: So what do you do?

AGNES: I talk to God. *He* doesn't frighten me.

DOCTOR: Is that why you're a nun?

AGNES: I suppose so. I couldn't live without Him.

DOCTOR: But don't you think God works through other religions, and other ways of life?

AGNES: I don't know.

DOCTOR: Couldn't I talk to Him?

AGNES: You could try. I don't know if He'd listen to *you*.

DOCTOR: Why not?

AGNES: Because you don't listen to Him.

DOCTOR: Agnes, have you ever thought of leaving the convent? For something else?

AGNES: Oh no. There's nothing else. It makes me happy. Just being here helps me sleep at night.

DOCTOR: You have trouble sleeping?

AGNES: I get headaches. Mummy did too. She'd lie in the dark with a wet cloth over her face and tell me to go away. Oh, but she wasn't stupid. Oh no, she was very smart. She knew everything. She even knew things nobody else knew.

DOCTOR: What things?

AGNES: The future. She knew what was going to happen to me, and that's why she hid me away. I didn't mind that. I didn't like school very much. And I liked being with Mummy. She'd tell me all kinds of things. She told me I would enter the convent, and I did. She even knew about this.

DOCTOR: This?

AGNES: This.

DOCTOR: Me?

AGNES: This.

DOCTOR: How did she know . . . about this?

AGNES: Somebody told her.

DOCTOR: Who?

AGNES: I don't know.

DOCTOR: Agnes.

AGNES: You'll laugh.

DOCTOR: I promise I won't laugh. Who told her?

AGNES: An angel. When she was having one of her head-aches. Before I was born.

DOCTOR: Did your mother see angels often?

AGNES: No. Only when she had her headaches. And not even then, sometimes.

DOCTOR: Do you see angels?

AGNES: (*A little too quickly*) No.

DOCTOR: Do you believe that your mother really saw them?

AGNES: No. But I could never tell her that.

DOCTOR: Why not?

AGNES: She'd get angry. She'd punish me.

DOCTOR: How would she punish you?

AGNES: She'd . . . punish me.

DOCTOR: Did you love your mother?

AGNES: Oh, yes. Yes.

DOCTOR: Did you ever want to become a mother yourself?

AGNES: I could never be a mother.

DOCTOR: Why not?

AGNES: I don't think I'm old enough. Besides, I don't want a baby.

DOCTOR: Why not?

AGNES: Because I don't want one.

DOCTOR: But if you did want one, how would you go about getting one?

AGNES: I'd adopt it.

DOCTOR: Where would the adopted baby come from?

AGNES: From an agency.

DOCTOR: Before the agency.

AGNES: From someone who didn't want a baby.

DOCTOR: Like you?

AGNES: No! Not like me.

DOCTOR: But how would that person get the baby if they didn't want it?

AGNES: A mistake.

DOCTOR: How did your mother get you?

AGNES: A mistake! It was a mistake!

DOCTOR: Is that what she said?

AGNES: You're trying to get me to say that she was a bad woman, and that she hated me, and she didn't want me, but that is not true, because she did love me, and she was a good woman, a saint, and she *did* want me. You don't want to hear the nice parts about her—all you're interested in is sickness!

DOCTOR: Agnes, I cannot imagine that you know nothing about sex . . .

AGNES: I can't help it if I'm stupid.

DOCTOR: . . . that you have no idea who the father of your child was . . .

AGNES: They made it up!

DOCTOR: . . . that you have no remembrance of your impregnation . . .

AGNES: It's not my fault!

DOCTOR: . . . and that you don't believe that you carried a child!

AGNES: It was a mistake!

DOCTOR: What, the child?

AGNES: Everything! Nuns don't have children!

DOCTOR: Agnes . . .

AGNES: Don't touch me like that! Don't touch me like that! (*Agnes lashes out at the doctor, who moves away*) I know what you want from me! You want to take God away. You should be ashamed! They should lock *you* up. People like you!

ACT I
Scene 8

MOTHER: You hate us, don't you?

DOCTOR: What?

MOTHER: Nuns. You hate nuns.

DOCTOR: I don't . . . (understand what you're talking about.)

MOTHER: Catholicism, then.

DOCTOR: I hate ignorance and stupidity.

MOTHER: And the Catholic Church.

DOCTOR: I haven't said . . . (anything about the Catholic Church.)

MOTHER: This is a human being you're dealing with, not an institution.

DOCTOR: But . . . (the institution has a hell of a lot to do with the human being.)

MOTHER: Catholicism is not on trial here. I want you to treat Agnes *without* any religious prejudices or turn this case over . . . (to another psychiatrist.)

DOCTOR: (*Exploding*) How dare you march into my office and tell me how to run my affairs—

MOTHER: It's my affair too.

DOCTOR: (*Overlapping*) . . . how dare you think that I'm in a position to be badgered . . .

MOTHER: I'm only requesting that . . . (you be fair.)

DOCTOR: (*Overlapping*) . . . or bullied or whatever you're trying to do. Who the hell do you think you are? You walk in here expecting applause for the way you've treated this child.

MOTHER: She's not a child.

DOCTOR: And she has a right to *know!* That there is a world out there filled with people who don't believe in God and who are not any worse off than you! People who go through their entire lives without bending their knees once —to *anybody!* And people who still fall in love, and make babies, and occasionally are very happy. She has a right to know that. But you, and your order, and your Church, have kept her ignorant . . .

MOTHER: We could hardly do that . . . (even if we wanted to.)

DOCTOR: . . . because ignorance is next to virginity, right? Poverty, chastity, and ignorance, that's what you live by.

MOTHER: I am not a virgin, Doctor. I was married for twenty-three years. Two daughters. I even have grandchildren. Surprised?
(*Silence*)
It might please you to know that I was a failure as a wife and mother. Possibly because I protected my children from

nothing. Out of the womb and into the "big bad world." They won't see me anymore. That's their revenge. They're both devout atheists. I think they tell their friends I've passed on. Oh don't tell me, Doctor Freud, I'm making up for past mistakes.

DOCTOR: You can help her.

MOTHER: I am.

DOCTOR: No, you're shielding her. *Let* her face the big bad world.

MOTHER: Meaning you.

DOCTOR: Yes, if that's what you think.

MOTHER: What good would it do? No matter what you decide, it's either the prison or the nuthouse, and the differences between them are pretty thin.

DOCTOR: There's another choice.

MOTHER: What's that?

DOCTOR: Acquittal.

MOTHER: How?

DOCTOR: Innocence. Legal innocence. I'm sure the judge would be happy for *any* reason to throw this case out of court.

(*Silence*)

MOTHER: What do you want?

DOCTOR: Answers.

MOTHER: Ask.

DOCTOR: When would Sister Agnes have conceived the child?

MOTHER: About a year ago.

DOCTOR: You don't remember anything unusual happening at
the convent around that time?

MOTHER: Earthquakes?

DOCTOR: Visitors.

MOTHER: Nothing. She was singing a lot more then, but—oh,
dear God.

DOCTOR: What is it?

MOTHER: The sheets.

DOCTOR: What about the sheets?

MOTHER: I should have known, dear God, I should have suspected something.

DOCTOR: What do you mean?

MOTHER: Her sheets. Her sheets had disappeared. One of the
sisters complained to me about it. So I called her in.
(*Agnes appears*)
Sister Margaret says you've been sleeping on a bare mattress,
Sister. Is that true?

AGNES: Yes, Mother.

MOTHER: Why?

AGNES: In medieval days nuns and monks would sleep in
their coffins.

MOTHER: We're not in the Middle Ages, Sister.

AGNES: It made them holy.

MOTHER: It made them uncomfortable. If they didn't sleep well, I'm certain the next day they were cranky as mules.

AGNES: Yes, Mother.

MOTHER: Sister, where are your sheets?
(*Silence*)
Do you really believe sleeping on a bare mattress is the equivalent of sleeping in a coffin?

AGNES: No.

MOTHER: Then tell me. Where are your sheets?

AGNES: I burned them.

MOTHER: Why?

AGNES: They were stained.

MOTHER: Sister, how many times have *I* burned into your thick skull and all the other thick skulls of your fellow novices that menstruation is a perfectly natural process and nothing to be ashamed of?

AGNES: Yes, Mother.

MOTHER: Say it.

AGNES: It is a perfectly natural process and nothing to be ashamed of.

MOTHER: Mean it.

AGNES: It is a perfectly . . . (*Agnes begins to cry*)

MOTHER: A few years ago one of our sisters came to me, in tears, asking for comfort. Comfort because she was too old to have children. Not that she intended to, but once a month she had been reminded of the possibility of Motherhood. So dry your eyes, Sister, and thank God that He has filled you with that possibility.

AGNES: It's not that. It's not that.

MOTHER: What do you mean?

AGNES: It's not my time of the month.

MOTHER: Should you see a doctor?

AGNES: I don't know. I don't know what happened, Mother. I woke up and there was blood on the sheets, but I don't understand what happened. I don't know what I did wrong. I don't know why I should be punished.

MOTHER: For what?

AGNES: I don't know!

MOTHER: Sister?

AGNES: I don't know! I don't know!

MOTHER: Agnes?

AGNES: I don't know.

MOTHER: Sing something, will you? With me? What's your favorite? "Virgin Mary had one Son . . ."

AGNES: I don't . . .

MOTHER:
"Oh, oh, pretty little baby,
 Oh, oh, oh, pretty little baby . . ."

AGNES: I don't know.

MOTHER:
"Glory be to the new-born King."

AGNES: I don't know.

MOTHER:
"Some call Him Jesus,
 I think I'll call Him Savior . . ."

MOTHER and AGNES:
"Oh, oh, I think I'll call Him Savior,
 Oh, oh, oh, I think I'll call Him Savior,
 Glory be to the new-born King."

AGNES: (*Continuing under the next lines*)
"Virgin Mary had one Son,
 Oh, oh, pretty little baby,
 Oh, oh, oh, pretty little baby,
 Glory be to the new-born King."

MOTHER: I sent her to her room. She was calm by then. Said it was nothing. Wouldn't see a doctor. But I should have known.

DOCTOR: Known what?

MOTHER: That was the beginning. That was the night it happened. That is why she burned the sheets.

DOCTOR: What else do you remember about that night?

MOTHER: I'm not certain what night it was.

DOCTOR: Can you find out?

MOTHER: I keep a daybook at the convent.

DOCTOR: And can you check on any unusual activity around that time? You know, earthquakes and visitors?

MOTHER: I'll look in my daybook.

ACT I
Scene 9

DOCTOR: A psychiatrist and a nun died and went to heaven. At the pearly gates, Saint Peter asked them to fill out an application, which they did. Upon looking at their papers, he said, "I see you both were born on the same day in the same year." "Yes," said the doctor. "And that you have the same parents." "Yes," said the nun. "And so you're sisters." The nun smiled knowingly but it was the doctor who answered, "Yes." "And you must be twins," said the saint. "Oh, no," the two of them said, "we're not twins." "Same birthday, same parents, sisters, but not twins?" "Yes," they answered, and smiled.

I found this riddle, casually and coincidentally, on page 33 of an ancient issue of a defunct magazine. By this time, I was convinced that Agnes was completely innocent. I had begun to believe that someone else had murdered her child. Who that person was, and how I was to prove it, were riddles of my *own* making that I alone could solve. But the only answer I could come up with was upside down on page 117. (*Silence*) They were two of a set of triplets.

My problem was twofold: I wanted to free Agnes—legally prove her innocence—and I wanted to make her well.

AGNES: I'm not sick!

ACT I
Scene 10

DOCTOR: But you're troubled, aren't you?

AGNES: That's because you keep reminding me. If you go away, then I'll forget.

DOCTOR: And you're unhappy.

AGNES: Everybody's unhappy! You're unhappy, aren't you?

DOCTOR: Agnes.

AGNES: Aren't you?

DOCTOR: Sometimes, yes.

AGNES: Only you think you're lucky because you didn't have a mother who said things to you and did things that maybe weren't always nice, but that's what you think, because you don't know that my mother was a wonderful person, and even if you did know that you wouldn't believe it because you think she was bad, don't you.

DOCTOR: Agnes.

AGNES: Answer me! You never answer me!

DOCTOR: Yes, I do think your mother was wrong, sometimes.

AGNES: But that was because of me! Because *I* was bad, not her!

DOCTOR: What did you do?

AGNES: I'm always bad.

DOCTOR: What do you do?

AGNES: (*In tears*) No!

DOCTOR: What do you do?

AGNES: I breathe!

DOCTOR: What did your mother do to you? (*Agnes shakes her head*) If you can't tell me, shake your head, yes or no. Did she hit you?
("*No.*")
Did she make you do something you didn't want to do?
("*Yes.*")
Did it make you uncomfortable to do this?
("*Yes.*")
Did it embarrass you?
("*Yes.*")
Did it hurt you?
("*Yes.*")
What did she make you do?

AGNES: No.

DOCTOR: You can tell me.

AGNES: I can't.

DOCTOR: She's dead, isn't she?

AGNES: Yes.

DOCTOR: She can't hurt you anymore.

AGNES: She can.

DOCTOR: How?

AGNES: She watches, she listens.

DOCTOR: Agnes, I don't believe that. Tell me. I'll protect you from her.

AGNES: She . . .

DOCTOR: Yes?

AGNES: She . . . makes me . . . take off my clothes and then . . .

DOCTOR: Yes?

AGNES: . . . she makes . . . fun of me.

DOCTOR: She tells you you're ugly?

AGNES: Yes.

DOCTOR: And that you're stupid.

AGNES: Yes.

DOCTOR: And you're a mistake.

AGNES: She says . . . my whole body . . . is a mistake.

DOCTOR: Why?

AGNES: Because she says . . . if I don't watch out . . . I'll have a baby.

DOCTOR: How does she know that?

AGNES: Her headaches.

DOCTOR: Oh yes.

AGNES: And then . . . she touches me.

DOCTOR: Where?

AGNES: Down there.
(*Silence*)
With her cigarette.
(*Silence*)
Please, Mummy. Don't touch me like that. I'll be good. I
won't be your bad baby anymore.
(*Silence. The doctor puts out her cigarette*)

DOCTOR: Agnes, dear, I want you to do something. I want
you to pretend that I'm your mother. I know that your
mother's dead, and you're grown up now, but I want you to
pretend for a moment that your mother has come back and
that I'm your mother. Only this time, I want you to tell me
what you're feeling. All right?

AGNES: I'm afraid.

DOCTOR: (*She takes Agnes' face in her hands*) Please. I want
to help you. Let me help you.

(*Silence*)

AGNES: All right.

DOCTOR: Agnes, you're ugly. What do you say to that?

AGNES: I don't know.

DOCTOR: Of course you do. Agnes, you're ugly.
(*Silence*)
What do you say?

AGNES: No, I'm not.

DOCTOR: Are you pretty?

AGNES: Yes.

DOCTOR: Agnes, you're stupid.

AGNES: No, I'm not.

DOCTOR: Are you intelligent?

AGNES: Yes, I am.

DOCTOR: Agnes, you're a mistake.

AGNES: I'm not a mistake! I'm here, aren't I? How can I be a
mistake if I'm really here? God doesn't make mistakes.
You're a mistake! I wish you were dead! (*Silence*)

DOCTOR: It's all right. Just pretend, right?
(*Agnes nods*)
Thank you.
(*Agnes begins to cry. The doctor takes her in her arms*)
Agnes, I'd like to ask a favor of you. You can say no, if you
don't like what I'm asking.

AGNES: What?

DOCTOR: I'd like permission to hypnotize you.

AGNES: Why?

DOCTOR: Because there are some things that you might be able to tell me under hypnosis that you aren't able to tell me now.

AGNES: Does Mother Miriam know about this?

DOCTOR: Mother Miriam loves you very much just as I love you very much. I'm certain that she wouldn't object . . . (to anything that would help you.)

AGNES: Do you really love me? Or are you just saying that?

DOCTOR: I really love you.

AGNES: As much as Mother Miriam loves me?

(*Silence*)

DOCTOR: As much as God loves you.

(*Silence*)

AGNES: All right.

DOCTOR: Thank you. (*Doctor embraces Agnes. Mother enters, and watches them in silence*)

MOTHER: I brought the daybook.

DOCTOR: Agnes, you can go now. (*Agnes rises, bows before Mother for her blessing, exits*)
(*Lighting a cigarette*) What did you find?

MOTHER: What did *you* find?

DOCTOR: Some facts about her mother.

MOTHER: She wasn't exactly the healthiest of women, was she? Of course I can't speak for her *mental* health, but physically . . .

DOCTOR: You knew her?

MOTHER: We corresponded before her death.

DOCTOR: How old was Agnes when her mother died?

MOTHER: Seventeen.

DOCTOR: Why was she sent to you?

MOTHER: Her mother requested . . . (she be sent to us.)

DOCTOR: Why wasn't she sent to next of kin?

MOTHER: She was. Agnes' mother was my younger sister.

(*Silence*)

DOCTOR: You lied to me.

MOTHER: About what?

DOCTOR: You said you never saw Agnes until she set foot in the convent.

MOTHER: I didn't. I was a good deal older than my sister. In fact, I was already married before she was born. She was the proverbial black sheep. She ran away from home at an early age. We lost touch with her. When my husband died and I entered the convent, she started writing to me again. She told me about Agnes, and asked me to watch over her in case anything happened.

DOCTOR: And Agnes' father?

MOTHER: Could have been any one of a dozen men, from what my sister told me. She was afraid that Agnes would follow in her footsteps. She did everything to prevent that.

DOCTOR: By keeping her home from school.

MOTHER: Yes.

DOCTOR: And listening to angels.

MOTHER: She drank too much. That's what killed her.

DOCTOR: Do you know what she did to Agnes?

MOTHER: I don't think I . . . (care to know.)

DOCTOR: She molested her.

(*Silence*)

MOTHER: Oh dear Jesus.

DOCTOR: There *is* more here than meets the eye, isn't there? *Lots* of dirty little secrets. Pull back the sheets and what do you find? A niece.

MOTHER: I didn't tell you because I didn't think it was important.

DOCTOR: No, it just makes you doubly responsible, doesn't it? Blood runs thicker, right?

MOTHER: Had I known what Agnes was suffering . . .

DOCTOR: Why didn't you?! My God, you knew she was keeping the child from school. You knew she was an alcoholic.

MOTHER: I knew that *after* . . . (the fact.)

DOCTOR: Why didn't you do anything to stop her?

MOTHER: I didn't know! And that's no answer, is it?

(*Silence*)

DOCTOR: What did you find in the daybook?

MOTHER: Agnes was sick the Sunday before she told me about the sheets. If she burned them then, they probably became stained on Saturday night. Unfortunately, on that night one of our elder nuns passed away. I have no recollection of any visitors to the convent. I was needed in the sickroom.

DOCTOR: Was Extreme Unction given on that night?

MOTHER: Yes, of course.

DOCTOR: So Father Marshall would have been present.

MOTHER: Yes, but you can't believe . . . (that Father Marshall could have done it.)

DOCTOR: Somebody has to be responsible for that child. If it wasn't Father Marshall, who else could it be?
(*Silence*)
Well, we'll find out soon enough. I've gotten Agnes' permission to hypnotize her.

MOTHER: And *my* permission?

DOCTOR: I don't think you have anything to say in this matter.

MOTHER: I'm her guardian.

DOCTOR: She's twenty-one years old; she doesn't need a guardian.

MOTHER: But she must come to me first and ask permission.

DOCTOR: Does this mean you'll deny it?

MOTHER: I haven't decided that yet.

DOCTOR: This woman's health is at stake.

MOTHER: Her spiritual health.

DOCTOR: I don't give a good goddamn about what you call . . . (her spiritual health.)

MOTHER: I know you don't.

DOCTOR: Sentence her and be done with it, that's what you're saying. Well, *I* can't . . . (do that yet.)

MOTHER: What I'm saying is that you have a beautifully simple woman . . .

DOCTOR: An unhappy woman.

MOTHER: But she was happy with us. And she could go on being happy if she were left alone.

DOCTOR: Then why did you call the police in the first place? Why didn't you throw the baby in the incinerator and be done with it?

MOTHER: Because I'm a moral person, that's why.

DOCTOR: Bullshit!

MOTHER: Bullshit yourself!

DOCTOR: The Catholic Church doesn't have a corner on morality, Mother.

MOTHER: Who said anything about the Catholic Church?

DOCTOR: You just said . . . (that you . . .)

MOTHER: What the hell does the Catholic Church have to do with you?

DOCTOR: Nothing. Absolutely nothing.

MOTHER: What have we done to hurt you?

DOCTOR: (*Beginning to speak*) (Nothing.)

MOTHER: And don't deny it. Oh, I can smell an ex-Catholic a mile away. What did we do? Burn a few heretics? Sell some indulgences? But those were in the days when the Church was a ruling body. We let governments do those things today.

DOCTOR: Just because you don't have the power you once had . . .

MOTHER: Oh, I'm not interested in the Church as power, Doctor. I'm interested in it as simplicity and peace. I know, it's very difficult to find that in *any* institution nowadays. So tell me. What did we do to you? You wanted to neck in the back seat of a car when you were fifteen and you couldn't because it was a sin. So instead of questioning that one little rule—

DOCTOR: It wasn't sex. It was a lot of things, but it wasn't sex. It started in the first grade when my best friend was run over by a cement truck on her way to school. The nun said she died because she hadn't said her morning prayers.

MOTHER: Stupid woman.

DOCTOR: Yeah.

MOTHER: That's all?

DOCTOR: That's all?! That's enough. She was a *beautiful* little
girl . . . (and to explain away her death like that . . .)

MOTHER: What has that got to do with it?

DOCTOR: I wasn't! She was the pretty one, and she died. Why
not me? I hadn't said my morning prayers either. And I
was ugly. Not just plain. Ugly! I was fat,* I had big buck
teeth, ears out to here, and freckles all over my face. Sister
Mary Cletus used to call me PolkaDot Livingstone. (*The
doctor is laughing in spite of herself*)

MOTHER: So you left the Church because you had freckles?

DOCTOR: No, because . . . Yeah, I left the Church because I
had freckles. And guess what?

MOTHER: What?

DOCTOR: (*Smiling*) That's also why I hate nuns.

(*Agnes is heard singing, then humming until indicated*)

AGNES: *Sanctus, sanctus, sanctus,*
Dominus Deus Sabaoth.
Pleni sunt coeli et terra gloria tua.

Hosanna in excelsis.
Benedictus qui venit in nomine Domini.
Hosanna in excelsis.

* or scrawny

DOCTOR: Why is that so important to you, her singing?

MOTHER: When I was a child I used to speak with my guardian angel. Oh, I don't ask you to believe that I heard loud, miraculous voices, but just as some children have invisible playmates, I had angelic conversations. Like Agnes' mother, you might say, but I was a lot younger then, and I am not Agnes' mother. Anyway, when I was six I stopped listening and my angel stopped speaking. But just as a sailor remembers the sea, I remembered that voice. I grew, fell in love, married and was widowed, joined the convent, and shortly after I was chosen Mother Superior, I looked at myself one day and saw nothing but a survivor of an unhappy marriage, a mother of two angry daughters, and a nun who was certain of nothing. Not even of Heaven, Doctor Livingstone. Not even of God. And then one evening, while walking in a field beside the convent wall, I heard a voice and looking up I saw one of our new postulants standing in her window, singing. It was Agnes, and she was beautiful; and all of my doubts about God and myself vanished in that one moment. I recognized the voice. (*Silence*) Don't take it away from me again, Doctor Livingstone. Those years after six were very bleak.

DOCTOR: My sister died in a convent. And it's *her* voice *I* hear. (*Agnes stops singing. Silence*) Does my smoking still bother you?

MOTHER: No, it only reminds me.

DOCTOR: Would you like one?

MOTHER: I would love one, but no thank you.

DOCTOR: Once, years ago at the beginning of "the scare," I decided to stop. I had no idea how many cigarettes I smoked then, but I used a book of matches a day. So I came up with the ingenious plan of cutting back on matches. First a half book, then a quarter of a book, then down to three or four a day. And look at what happened. I can't even eat without a cigarette in my hand. I can't go to weddings or funerals, plays, concerts. But some days I can go fourteen hours on a single match. Remarkable, isn't it? Do you think the saints would have smoked, had tobacco been popular?

MOTHER: Undoubtedly. Not the ascetics, of course, but, well, Saint Thomas More . . .

DOCTOR: Parliaments.

MOTHER: Saint Ignatius, I think, would smoke Camels and then stub them out on the soles of his feet. Of course all the Apostles—

DOCTOR: Hand-rolled.

MOTHER: Yes, and even Christ would partake socially.

DOCTOR: Saint Peter, the original Marlboro man.

MOTHER: Mary Magdalene?

DOCTOR: You've come a long way, baby.

MOTHER: Saint Joan would chew Mail Pouch.

DOCTOR: (*Taking a toke*) And what, do you suppose, are today's saints smoking?

MOTHER: There are no saints today. Good people, yes. But extraordinarily good people? I'm afraid those we are sorely lacking.

DOCTOR: Do you believe they ever existed, these extraordinarily good people?

MOTHER: Yes, I do.

DOCTOR: Would you like to become one?

MOTHER: To become? One is born a saint. Only no one is born a saint today. We've evolved too far. We're too complicated.

DOCTOR: But you can try, can't you? To be good?

MOTHER: Oh yes, but goodness has very little to do with it. Not all the saints were good. In fact, most of them were a little crazy. But their hearts were with God, left in His hands at birth. "Trailing clouds of glory." No more. We're born, we live, we die. Occasionally one might appear among us, still attached to God. But we cut that cord very quickly. No freaks here. We're all solid, sensible men and women, feet on the ground, money in the bank, innocence trampled underfoot. Our minds dissected, our bodies cut open, "No soul here; must have been a delusion." We look at the sky, "No God up there, no heaven, no hell." Well, we're better off. Less disease, for one thing. No *room* for miracles. But oh my dear, how I miss the miracles.

DOCTOR: Do you really believe miracles happened?

MOTHER: Of course I do. I believe in the miracle of the loaves and fishes two thousand years ago as strongly as I would doubt it today. What we've gained in logic we've lost in faith. We no longer have any sort of . . . primitive wonder. The closest we come to a miracle today is in bed. And we give up everything for it. Including those bits of light that might still, by the smallest chance, be clinging to our souls, reaching back to God.

DOCTOR: The saints had lovers.

MOTHER: Oh yes, the saints had lovers, but then the cord was a rope. Now it's a thread.

DOCTOR: Do you believe Agnes is still attached to God?

MOTHER: Listen to her singing.

DOCTOR: Time to begin.

MOTHER: Begin what?

DOCTOR: The hypnotism. You still disapprove?

MOTHER: Will it stop you if I do?

DOCTOR: No.

MOTHER: May I be present?

DOCTOR: Yes. Of course.

MOTHER: Then let's begin.

(*Blackout*)

INTERMISSION

ACT II

ACT II

Scene 1

AGNES: (*Singing*) *Basiez moy, ma doulce amye,*
Par amour je vous en prie
Non feray. Et pour quoy?
Se je faisoie la folie,
Ma mêre en seroit morrie.
Velâ de quoy, velâ de quoy.

DOCTOR: The hypnosis took weeks to achieve, not minutes. An hour a day, spaced in between a kleptomaniac and an exhibitionist. Between lunch and dinner. Between Phil Donahue and Dan Rather. Between sleepless nights. Endless weekends. But *my* memories, oh, *they* come *too* easily. Sometimes they won't even let me finish a sentence. They come galloping out, mid-thought. I know if only I could finish the thought, they would . . . (go away.)

ACT II

Scene 2

AGNES: I'm frightened!

DOCTOR: Don't be. I cannot make you say or do anything you do not wish to say or do. Sit back and relax. Fine. Now imagine that you are listening to a chorus of angels. Their music is so beautiful and so real that you can touch it. It surrounds you like a very warm and comfortable pool of water. The water is so warm you hardly know that it's there. All of the muscles in your body are melting into the pool. The water is just under your chin. But you must remember that this water is music, and if you are submersed in it you can still breathe freely and deeply. Now the water covers your chin. Your mouth, your nose, and your eyes. Close your eyes, Agnes. Thank you. When I count to three, you will wake up. Can you hear me?

AGNES: Yes.

DOCTOR: Who am I?

AGNES: Doctor Livingstone.

DOCTOR: And why am I here?

AGNES: To help me.

DOCTOR: Good. Would you like to tell me why you're here?

AGNES: Because I'm in trouble.

DOCTOR: What kind of trouble?
(*Silence*)
What kind of trouble, Agnes?

AGNES: I'm frightened.

DOCTOR: Of what?

AGNES: Of telling you.

DOCTOR: But it's easy. It's only a breath with sound. Say it.
What kind of trouble, Agnes?

(*Agnes struggles, then says:*)

AGNES: I had a baby.

(*Silence*)

DOCTOR: How did you have a baby?

AGNES: It came out of me.

DOCTOR: Did you know it was going to come out?

AGNES: Yes.

DOCTOR: Did you want it to come out?

AGNES: No.

DOCTOR: Why?

AGNES: Because I was afraid.

DOCTOR: Why were you afraid?

AGNES: Because I wasn't worthy.

DOCTOR: To be a mother?

AGNES: Yes.

DOCTOR: Why?

(*Agnes begins to cry softly*)

AGNES: May I open my eyes now?

DOCTOR: Not yet. Very soon, but not yet. Do you know how the baby got into you?

AGNES: It grew.

DOCTOR: What made it grow? Do you know?

AGNES: Yes.

DOCTOR: Would you like to tell me?

AGNES: No.

DOCTOR: Did you know from the beginning that you were going to have a baby?

AGNES: Yes.

DOCTOR: How did you know?

AGNES: I just knew.

DOCTOR: What did you do about it?

AGNES: I drank lots of milk.

DOCTOR: Why?

AGNES: Because that's good for babies.

DOCTOR: You wanted the baby to be healthy?

AGNES: Yes.

DOCTOR: Then why didn't you go to a doctor?

AGNES: Nobody would believe me.

DOCTOR: That you were having a baby?

AGNES: No, not that.

DOCTOR: What wouldn't they believe?
(*Silence*)
Agnes, did anyone else know about the baby?

AGNES: Yes.

DOCTOR: Who?

AGNES: I don't want to tell you.

DOCTOR: Did you tell this other person or did this other person guess?

AGNES: She guessed.

DOCTOR: One of your fellow sisters.

AGNES: Yes.

DOCTOR: Will she be angry if you tell me her name?

AGNES: She made me promise not to.

DOCTOR: All right, Agnes, I'm going to ask you to open your eyes in a moment. When you do, you will see your room at the convent. It is the night about four months ago when you were very sick. Around six o'clock in the evening.

AGNES: I'm afraid.

DOCTOR: Don't be. I'm here. All right?

AGNES: Yes.

DOCTOR: Now tell me what you did this evening before you went to bed.

AGNES: I ate.

DOCTOR: What did you have for dinner?

AGNES: Fish. Brussels sprouts.

DOCTOR: You don't like brussels sprouts?

AGNES: I hate them.

DOCTOR: What else?

AGNES: A little coffee. Some sherbet for dessert. That was special.

DOCTOR: And then what?

AGNES: We got up, cleared the table, and went to chapel for vespers.

DOCTOR: Yes?

AGNES: I left early because I wasn't feeling very well.

DOCTOR: What was wrong?

AGNES: Just tired. I had my milk . . . (and went to bed.)

DOCTOR: Who gave you your milk?

AGNES: Sister Margaret, I think.

DOCTOR: Was it Sister Margaret who knew about the baby?
(*Silence*)
All right, Agnes, let's go to your room. Ready?

AGNES: Yes.

DOCTOR: I want you to open your eyes, and to see your room
as you saw it on that night. What do you see?

AGNES: My bed.

DOCTOR: What else is in the room?

AGNES: A chair.

DOCTOR: Where is that?

AGNES: Here.

DOCTOR: Anything else?

AGNES: A crucifix.

DOCTOR: Above the bed?

AGNES: Yes.

DOCTOR: Anything else?
(*Silence*)
Agnes? What do you see? Something different?

AGNES: Yes.

DOCTOR: Something that's not normally in the room?

AGNES: Yes.

DOCTOR: What is that?

AGNES: A wastepaper basket.

(*Silence*)

DOCTOR: Do you know who put it there?

AGNES: No.

DOCTOR: Why do you think it's there?

AGNES: For me to get sick in.

DOCTOR: Are you ill?

AGNES: Yes.

DOCTOR: What do you feel?

AGNES: A pain in my stomach. I feel as if I've eaten glass. (*She holds her stomach in a contraction*)

DOCTOR: What do you do?

AGNES: I have to throw up. (*She tries*) I can't. (*Contraction*) It's glass! One of the sisters has fed me glass!

DOCTOR: Which one?

AGNES: I don't know which one. They're all jealous, that's why.

DOCTOR: Of what?

AGNES: Of me! (*Contraction*) Oh God. Oh my God. Water. It's all water!

DOCTOR: Why doesn't anyone come?

AGNES: They can't hear me.

DOCTOR: Why not?

AGNES: They're all in vespers.

DOCTOR: Can you get them?

AGNES: I can't. It's clear on the other side of the building. (*Contraction*) Oh no, please. Please. I don't want this to happen. I don't want it.

DOCTOR: Where are you?

AGNES: On the bed. (*Contraction*) Oh God. Oh my God. (*Sharp intake of breath*)

DOCTOR: What is it?

AGNES: Get away from me.

DOCTOR: Who?

AGNES: Go away! I don't want you here!

DOCTOR: Is someone in the room with you? Agnes?

AGNES: Don't touch me! Don't touch me! Please! Please don't touch me! (*Contraction*) No, I don't want to have the baby now. I don't want it! Why are you making me do this? (*Contraction. She begins to scream*)

DOCTOR: It's all right, Agnes. No one's going to hurt you.

AGNES: You want to hurt my baby! You want to take my baby! (*Contraction*)

MOTHER: Stop her, she'll hurt herself!

DOCTOR: No, let her go . . . (for a moment.)

MOTHER: (*Rushing to Agnes*) I'm not going on with this . . . (anymore.)

DOCTOR: No!

(*As Mother touches her, Agnes screams, striking Mother and pushing her away*)

AGNES: You're trying to take my baby! You're trying to take my baby! (*Scream and contraction*) Stay in! Please stay in! (*Several violent and final contractions*)

MOTHER: Stop her! Help her!

AGNES: BITCH! It's not my fault, Mummy. WHORE! It's a mistake, Mummy. LIAR!

DOCTOR: Agnes, it's all right. One, two, three. It's all right. (*Agnes relaxes*)
It's me. Doctor Livingstone. It's all right. Thank you. Thank you. How do you feel?

AGNES: Frightened.

DOCTOR: It's hard enough to go through it once, isn't it?

AGNES: Yes.

DOCTOR: Do you remember what just happened?

AGNES: Yes.

DOCTOR: Good. Do you think you're well enough to stand?

AGNES: Yes. (*She does*)

DOCTOR: There.

(*Agnes embraces the doctor. As she leaves, she begins to sing*)

AGNES: *Ave Maria,*
Gratia plena,
Dominus tecum.
Benedicta tu in mulieribus,
Et benedictus fructus ventris tui, Jesu.

MOTHER: You've formed your opinion about her, haven't you?

DOCTOR: She's a very disturbed young woman, but . . . (I don't feel that's all there is to it.)

MOTHER: Your job is done.

DOCTOR: As far as the court is concerned, yes, but personally—

MOTHER: Personally?! I don't think you were asked to become personally involved.

DOCTOR: But I am.

MOTHER: And I'm asking you to get the hell out! If we want to hire a psychiatrist for Agnes, we'll find our own, thank you.

DOCTOR: One who'll ask her the questions you want asked.

MOTHER: One who will approach this matter with some objectivity and respect!

DOCTOR: For you?!

MOTHER: For Agnes.

DOCTOR: You still believe that my interference will destroy some sort of . . . (special aura about her?)

MOTHER: She's a remarkable person, Doctor.

DOCTOR: That doesn't make her a saint.

MOTHER: I never said she was.

DOCTOR: But that's what you believe, isn't it?

MOTHER: That she's been touched by God, yes.

DOCTOR: Prove that to me! She sings—is that unique? She hallucinates, stops eating, and bleeds spontaneously. Is that supposed to convince me that she shouldn't be touched? I want a miracle! Nothing less. *Then* I'll leave her be.

(*Silence*)

MOTHER: The father.

DOCTOR: Who is he?

MOTHER: Why must he be anybody?

DOCTOR: (*Laughing*) You're as crazy as the rest of your family.

MOTHER: I don't know if it's true, I . . . (only think it might be possible.)

DOCTOR: How?

MOTHER: I don't . . . (know.)

DOCTOR: Do you think a big white dove came flying through her window?

MOTHER: No, I can't believe that.

DOCTOR: That would be a little scary, wouldn't it? Second Coming Stopped by Hysterical Nun.

MOTHER: This is *not* the Second Coming, Doctor Livingstone. Don't misunderstand me.

DOCTOR: But you just said . . . (there isn't any father.)

MOTHER: If this is true—and I mean *if*—it's nothing more than a slightly miraculous *scientific* event.

DOCTOR: Nothing more? Oh come on, Mother, you don't expect me to believe garbage . . . (like that.)

MOTHER: You can believe what you like. I only told you because . . . (you asked for a miracle.)

DOCTOR: If this is some miracle of science, there must be a reasonable explanation.

MOTHER: But a miracle is an event *without* an explanation. That's why people like you fail to believe, because you demand an explanation, and when you don't get one you create one.

DOCTOR: What the hell are you talking about?

MOTHER: Unanswered questions. Tiny discrepancies in what people like you say is the way of the world.

DOCTOR: This is insane.

MOTHER: The mind is a remarkable thing, Doctor Livingstone. You know that as well as I do. People bend spoons, stop watches. Zen archers split arrows down the center, one after another. We haven't *begun* to explore the mind's possibilities. If she's capable of putting a hole in her hand without benefit of a nail, why couldn't she split a tiny cell in her womb?

DOCTOR: Hysterical parthenogenesis, is that what you mean?

MOTHER: Partheno what?

DOCTOR: The female's ability in lower life forms to reproduce alone.

MOTHER: I don't pretend to . . . (understand it biologically.)

DOCTOR: If frogs can do it, why not Agnes.

MOTHER: Two thousand years ago, some people believe, a man was born without a father. Now no intelligent person today accepts that without question. We want answers, yes, that's the nature of science, but look at the answers we provide. An angel came to the woman in a shaft of light, hysterical parthenogenesis. If those are the answers, the answers are crazy. If those are the answers, no wonder people like you don't believe in miracles.

DOCTOR: The virgin birth was a lie told to a cuckolded husband by a frightened wife.

MOTHER: Oh, *that's* a plausible explanation. That's what you're looking for, right? Plausibility! But I believe that it is also the nature of science to wonder, and we can only wonder if we are willing to question *without* finding all the answers.

DOCTOR: But we *can* find them.

MOTHER: You can *look* for them. There's a difference. There was *no* man at the convent on that night, and there was *no* way for any man to get in or out.

DOCTOR: So you're saying God did it.

MOTHER: No! That's as much as saying Father Marshall did it. I'm saying God permitted it.

DOCTOR: But how did it happen?

MOTHER: You'll never find the answer to everything, Doctor. One and one is two, yes, but that leads to four and then to eight and soon to infinity. The wonder of science is not in the answers it provides but in the questions it uncovers. For every miracle it finally explains, ten thousand more miracles come into being.

DOCTOR: I thought you didn't believe in miracles today?

MOTHER: But I *want* to believe. I want the *opportunity* to believe. I want the *choice* to believe.

DOCTOR: What you are choosing to believe is a lie. Because you don't want to face the fact that she was raped, or seduced, or that *she* did the seducing.

MOTHER: She is an innocent.

DOCTOR: But she's not an enigma. Everything that Agnes has done is explainable by modern psychiatry. She's an hysteric. She was molested as a child. She had no father, an alcoholic mother. She was locked in a house until she was seventeen and in a convent until she was twenty-one. One-two-three, right down the line.

MOTHER: Is that what you believe, that she's the sum of her psychological parts?

DOCTOR: That's what I *have* to believe.

MOTHER: Then why are you so obsessed with her?
(*Silence*)
You're losing sleep, thinking of her all the time, bent on saving her. Why? That's a question, no answer needed. I'm not accusing, I'm recognizing. The symptoms are very familiar. *I* know. I'm an expert on the disease. We're in this together, you and I.

(*Silence*)

DOCTOR: So you believe that God permitted her . . .

MOTHER: Possibly.

DOCTOR: Possibly permitted her to have a child . . .

MOTHER: Not divine.

DOCTOR: Not divine, just a child, without benefit of man.

MOTHER: That's what I would like to believe, yes.

DOCTOR: Without proof?

MOTHER: Definitely without proof. There's no infallible proof for virginity. Only an absence of proof against it.

DOCTOR: Then how do you explain the bloody sheets on the night of the conception?

MOTHER: I can't.

DOCTOR: And why did the baby die?

MOTHER: I don't . . . (know.)

DOCTOR: Do you think God made a mistake and tried to correct it?

MOTHER: Don't be . . . (absurd.)

DOCTOR: Or is this all a hoax, a cover-up, to lead me down the garden path?

MOTHER: Why would I want to do that?

DOCTOR: Because this is murder we're talking about.

MOTHER: Murder?

DOCTOR: You believe Agnes is innocent. Well, I believe she's innocent too—of this crime. Like you, I have no proof. But I'm looking, and if it's there, I'll find it.

MOTHER: Don't try to turn this into some kind of murder mystery, Doctor.

DOCTOR: Aren't you concerned about what she just told us? About that other person in the room?

MOTHER: I'm concerned about her . . . (health and her safety.)

DOCTOR: Who *was* that other person, Mother? Was it you?!

MOTHER: If you persist in believing that this is a case of murder, then it is the district attorney you must consult, not me. And definitely not Agnes. (*Mother turns to leave*)

DOCTOR: Where are you going?

MOTHER: To the court. To have you taken off this case.

DOCTOR: Why? Am I getting too close . . . (to the truth?)

MOTHER: Doctor, I pray that—

DOCTOR: Agnes is innocent, isn't she?

MOTHER: (*Overlapping*)—someday you may understand my position.

DOCTOR: *Isn't she?*

MOTHER: Good-bye, Doctor. Oh, and as for that miracle you wanted, it *has* happened. It's a very small one, but you'll notice it soon enough. (*Mother leaves. Agnes enters*)

AGNES: You were fighting.

DOCTOR: (*Quickly and secretly*) Agnes, listen. You must help me. Has Mother Miriam ever threatened you in any way?

AGNES: No.

DOCTOR: Or frightened you?

AGNES: Why are you asking that?

DOCTOR: Because I believe she . . . (may have something to do with—)

MOTHER: (*Offstage*) Sister Agnes!

AGNES: Coming, Mother!

DOCTOR: Agnes, who . . . (was in the room with you?)

AGNES: I won't see you again, will I?

DOCTOR: Yes, you will. I promise. Agnes, who was in the room with you?
(*Silence*)
Do you know?

AGNES: Yes.

DOCTOR: Who was it? For the love of God, tell me.

AGNES: It was my mother.

MOTHER: (*Offstage*) Agnes!

AGNES: Good-bye. (*Agnes leaves*)

ACT II

Scene 3

DOCTOR: I dreamt that night that I was a midwife in a small private hospital in a faraway land. I was dressed in white and the room I was in was white, and a window was open and I could see mountains of snow all around. Below me on a table lay a woman prepared for a cesarean. She began to scream and I knew I had to cut the baby out as quickly as possible. I slipped a knife into her belly, then reached to my wrists inside. Suddenly I felt a tiny hand grab hold of my finger and begin to pull, and the woman's hands pressed down on my head, and the little creature inside drew me in, to the elbows, to the shoulders, to the chin, but when I opened my mouth to scream—I woke up, to find my sheets spotted. With blood. *My* blood. My rather sporadic menstrual cycle had ceased altogether some three years before, but on that night it began again.

(*Silence*)

What would I have done with a child? Nothing. Nothing.

(*Silence*)

The next day I asked for and received an order from the court allowing Agnes to return to my care. You see, I was so sure I was right. As a doctor, perhaps, I should have known better, but as a person—(*She begins to beat her chest with her fist*)

I am not made of granite. I am made of flesh and blood . . . and heart . . . and soul. . . . (*She continues to beat her chest in silence for a few moments, then stops*)

This is it. The unfinished thought. The last reel. No alternate in sight.

ACT II
Scene 4

MOTHER: Well, you've won, haven't you?

DOCTOR: Not at all, not yet.

MOTHER: You've decided to take . . . (her apart.)

DOCTOR: I've decided to hypnotize her again.

MOTHER: Hasn't she had enough?

DOCTOR: And I want to ask you a few questions that I wasn't able to ask you before . . .

MOTHER: I'm all ears.

DOCTOR: . . . because you very cleverly steered away from them.

MOTHER: My God, but you're vindictive.

DOCTOR: You're hiding something from me and I want to know the truth.

MOTHER: Then ask.

DOCTOR: Did Agnes ever say anything to you about not feeling well, while she was carrying the child?

MOTHER: Yes, she did.

DOCTOR: Then why didn't you send her to a doctor?

MOTHER: She wouldn't go.

DOCTOR: Wouldn't she?

MOTHER: No, she was afraid.

DOCTOR: Of what? That he might find something out? Is that what she told you? Or did you guess that?

MOTHER: If you're going to continue to persecute me . . . (I'll stop this conversation immediately.)

DOCTOR: I'm not persecuting you; I'm asking you a question.

MOTHER: I'm a nun, and you hate . . . (nuns.)

DOCTOR: Did you know that she was pregnant?!

(*Silence. Mother desperately tries to fight back and hide her tears. Then she speaks*)

MOTHER: Yes.

DOCTOR: And you didn't send her to a doctor?

MOTHER: It was too late.

DOCTOR: What do you mean?

MOTHER: I didn't guess it until—(*Silence. Mother fights for control*)

DOCTOR: Until when? Don't waste those tears on me, Mother. Until when?

MOTHER: Until it was too late.

DOCTOR: For what? An abortion?

MOTHER: Don't be absurd.

DOCTOR: Too late for what?!

MOTHER: I don't know, too late to stop it!

DOCTOR: The baby?

MOTHER: The scandal! It was too late to stop it but I had to try. I had to keep it quiet. I made her promise not to tell anyone. I had to have time to think.

DOCTOR: And you didn't get it, did you?

MOTHER: No! That night when she was ill, I knew . . .

DOCTOR: That time had run out?

MOTHER: Yes.

DOCTOR: So you went to her room to help her with the birth.

MOTHER: She didn't want help.

DOCTOR: But *you* wanted the child out of the way as quickly as possible.

MOTHER: That's a lie.

DOCTOR: You hid the wastepaper basket in the room.

MOTHER: I didn't hide it! I put it there for the blood and the dirty sheets . . .

DOCTOR: And the baby.

MOTHER: No!

DOCTOR: You tied the cord around its neck . . .

MOTHER: I simply wanted her to have it when no one was around. I would have taken the baby to a hospital and left it with them. But there was so much blood, I panicked.

DOCTOR: Before or after you killed the child?

MOTHER: I left it with her! I went for help!

DOCTOR: I doubt that's what she'll say.

MOTHER: Then she's a goddamn liar! (*Mother covers her face with her hands. Agnes is heard singing*)

AGNES: *Agnus Dei,*
qui tollis peccata mundi,
miserere nobis.
Agnus Dei,
qui tollis peccata mundi,
miserere nobis.
Agnus Dei,
qui tollis peccata mundi,
dona nobis pacem.

MOTHER: All right. Let's finish this once and for all. (*Mother exits. She gently takes Agnes' face between her hands. Alone, the doctor begins to cross herself, but stops. Agnes enters, followed by Mother*)

DOCTOR: Hello, Agnes.

AGNES: Hello.

DOCTOR: I have some more questions I'd like to ask you. Is that all right?

AGNES: Yes.

DOCTOR: And I would like to hypnotize you again. Is that all right too?

AGNES: Yes.

DOCTOR: Good. Sit down. Relax. You're going to enter the pool of water again. Only this time, I want you to imagine that there are holes in your body, and the warm water is flowing into those holes, behind your eyes, warm, so warm, so clean, like prayer, your eyes are so heavy, so . . . sleepy. Close your eyes. When I count to three, you'll wake up. Agnes, can you hear me?

AGNES: Yes.

DOCTOR: Who am I?

AGNES: Doctor Livingstone.

DOCTOR: And who is with me?

AGNES: Mother Miriam Ruth.

DOCTOR: Fine. Now Agnes, I'm going to ask you a few questions, and I'd like you to keep your eyes closed. All right?

AGNES: Yes.

DOCTOR: I would like you to remember, if you can, one night about a year ago, a Saturday night, when one of the sisters in the convent died.

MOTHER: Sister Paul.

DOCTOR: The night when Sister Paul died. Do you remember?

AGNES: Yes.

DOCTOR: What's the matter?

AGNES: I liked Sister Paul.

DOCTOR: Agnes, what happened that night?

AGNES: She sent me to bed early.

DOCTOR: Who did?

AGNES: Mother.

DOCTOR: Did you go to bed?

AGNES: Yes.

DOCTOR: Imagine that you are in your room, Agnes. Tell us what happened.

AGNES: I woke up.

DOCTOR: What time is it?

AGNES: I don't know. It's still dark.

DOCTOR: Do you see anything?

AGNES: Not at first. But . . .

DOCTOR: What?

AGNES: Someone is in the room.

DOCTOR: Are you frightened?

AGNES: Yes.

DOCTOR: What do you do?
(*Silence*)
Agnes?

AGNES: Who is it?
(*Silence*)
Who's there?
(*Silence*)
Is it you?
(*Silence*)
But I *am* afraid.
(*Silence*)
Yes.
(*Silence*)
Yes I do.
(*Silence*)
Why me?
(*Silence*)
Wait. I want to see you! (*She gasps and opens her eyes*)

DOCTOR: What do you see?

AGNES: A flower. Waxy and white. A drop of blood, sinking into the petal, flowing through the veins. A tiny halo. Millions of halos, dividing and dividing, feathers are stars, falling, falling into the iris of God's eye. Oh my God, he sees me. Oh, it's so lovely, so blue, yellow, green leaves brown blood, no, red, His Blood, my God, my God, I'm bleeding, I'M BLEEDING! (*She is bleeding from the palms of her hands*)

MOTHER: Oh my God.

AGNES: I have to wash this off, it's on my hands, my legs, my God, it's on the sheets, help me clean the sheets, help me, help me, it won't come out, the blood won't come out!

MOTHER: (*Grabbing her*) Agnes . . .

AGNES: Let go of me!

MOTHER: Agnes, please . . .

AGNES: You wanted this to happen, didn't you?! You prayed for this to happen, didn't you?!

MOTHER: No, I didn't.

AGNES: Get away from me! I don't want you anymore! I wish you were dead!

DOCTOR: Agnes . . .

AGNES: I wish you were all dead!

DOCTOR: . . . we had nothing to do with that man in your room.

AGNES: Let me alone!

DOCTOR: Do you understand? He did a very bad thing to you.

AGNES: Don't touch me!

DOCTOR: He frightened you, and he hurt you.

AGNES: Don't!

DOCTOR: It's not your fault . . .

AGNES: Mummy!

DOCTOR: . . . it's his fault.

AGNES: Mummy's fault!

DOCTOR: Tell us who he is so we can find him . . .

AGNES: (*To Mother*) Your fault!

DOCTOR: . . . and stop him from doing this to other women.

AGNES: (*To Mother*) It's all your fault!

DOCTOR: Agnes, who did you see in the room?!

AGNES: I hate him.

DOCTOR: Of course you do. Who was he?

AGNES: I hate him for what he did to me.

DOCTOR: Yes.

AGNES: For what he made me go through.

DOCTOR: Who?

AGNES: I hate him!

DOCTOR: Who did this to you?

AGNES: God! God did it to me! It was God! And now I'll burn in hell because I hate Him!

DOCTOR: Agnes, you won't burn in hell. It's all right to hate him.

MOTHER: That's enough for today, wake her up.

DOCTOR: Not yet.

MOTHER: She's tired and she's not well, and *I'm* taking her home.

DOCTOR: She doesn't belong to you anymore.

MOTHER: She belongs to God.

DOCTOR: She belongs to *me,* and she's staying here!

MOTHER: You can't . . . (keep her here.)

DOCTOR: Agnes, what happened to the baby?

MOTHER: She can't remember!

DOCTOR: Yes she can! Agnes . . .

MOTHER: She doesn't remember!

DOCTOR: (*Grabbing Agnes*) . . . what happened to the baby?!

AGNES: They threw it away.

DOCTOR: No, after the birth.

AGNES: It was dead.

MOTHER: Don't do this to her!

DOCTOR: It was alive, wasn't it?

AGNES: I don't remember.

MOTHER: Please!

DOCTOR: It was alive, wasn't it?

MOTHER: Don't do this to *me!*

DOCTOR: *Wasn't it?*

AGNES: YES!!!

(*Silence*)

DOCTOR: What happened?

AGNES: I don't want to remember.

DOCTOR: But you do, don't you?

AGNES: Yes.

DOCTOR: Mother Miriam was with you, wasn't she?

AGNES: Yes.

DOCTOR: She took the baby in her arms . . .

AGNES: Yes.

DOCTOR: You saw it all, didn't you?

AGNES: Yes.

DOCTOR: And then . . . what did she do?
(*Silence*)
Agnes, what did she do?

AGNES: (*Simply and quietly*) She left me alone with that little
. . . thing. I looked at it and thought, this is a mistake. But
it's my mistake, not Mummy's. God's mistake. I thought, I
can save her. I can give her back to God.

(*Silence*)

DOCTOR: What did you do?

AGNES: I put her to sleep.

DOCTOR: How?

AGNES: I tied the cord around her neck, wrapped her in the bloody sheets, and stuffed her in the trash can.

MOTHER: No. (*Mother turns away. Silence*)

DOCTOR: One. Two. Three.
(*Agnes slowly rises and walks away, humming "Charlie's Neat" softly to herself*)
Mother?
(*Silence*)
Mother, please . . .

(*Mother turns to face the doctor*)

MOTHER: You were right. She remembered. And all this time I thought she was some unconscious innocent. Thank you, Doctor Livingstone. We need people like you to destroy all those lies that ignorant folk like myself pretend to believe.

DOCTOR: Mother . . .

MOTHER: But I'll never forgive you for what you've taken away.
(*Silence*)
You should have died. Not your sister. You.

AGNES: (*Speaking to an unseen friend*) Why are you crying?
(*The doctor and the Mother turn to her. Silence*)
But *I* believe. I *do*.
(*Silence*)
Please, don't you leave me too. Oh no. Oh my God, O sweet Lady, don't leave me. Please, please don't leave me. I'll be good. I won't be your bad baby anymore.
(*She sees someone else*)

No, Mummy. I don't want to go with you. Stop pulling me.
Your hands are hot. Don't touch me like that! Oh my God,
Mummy, don't burn me! DON'T BURN ME!
(*Silence. She turns to Mother and the doctor and stretches
out her hands like a statue of the Lady, showing her
bleeding palms. She smiles, and speaks simply and sanely*)
I stood in the window of my room every night for a week.
And one night I heard the most beautiful voice imaginable.
It came from the middle of the wheat field beyond my
room, and when I looked I saw the moon shining down on
Him. For six nights He sang to me. Songs I'd never heard.
And on the seventh night He came to my room and opened
His wings and lay on top of me. And all the while He sang.
(*Smiling and crying, she sings*)

"Charlie's neat and Charlie's sweet,
    And Charlie he's a dandy,
    Every time he goes to town,
    He gets his girl some candy.
    Over the river and through the trees,
    Over the river to Charlie's,
    Over the river and through the trees,
    To bake a cake for Charlie.
(*Mother begins to take Agnes off*)
"Charlie's neat and Charlie's sweet,
    And Charlie he's a dandy,
    Every time he goes to town,
    He gets his girl some candy.
    Oh, he gets his girl some candy."

ACT II
Scene 5

DOCTOR: (*Singing*) "Yes, he gets his girl some candy." I don't know the truth behind that song. Yes, perhaps it was a song of seduction, and the father was . . . a field hand. Or perhaps the song was simply a remembered lullaby sung many years before. And the father was . . . hope, and love, and desire, and a belief in miracles.

I never saw them again. The following day I removed myself from the case. Mother Miriam threw Agnes on the mercy of the court, and she was sent to a hospital . . . where she stopped singing . . . and eating . . . and where she died.

Why? Why was a child molested, and a baby killed, and a mind destroyed? Was it to the simple end that not two hours ago this doubting, menstruating, non-smoking psychiatrist made her confession? What kind of God can permit such a wonder one as her to come trampling through this well-ordered existence?!

I don't know what I believe anymore. But I *want* to believe that she was . . . blessed. And I *do* miss her. And I hope that she has left something, some little part of herself, with *me*. That would be miracle enough.

(*Silence*)

Wouldn't it?

Ⓜ   Ⓟ

More Great Plays From MERIDIAN CLASSICS and PLUME
                                                            (0452)
☐ **FIVE PLAYS BY MICHAEL WELLER.** With unmatched intimacy and
   accuracy, this remarkable collection of plays captures the feelings,
   the dilemmas, the stances, and above all the language of the 1980's.
   This volume brings together for the first time five of Weller's plays, in
   their author's final versions.   (253357—$8.95)

☐ **LORRAINE HANSBERRY, THE COLLECTED LAST PLAYS.** The three
   plays in this volume represent the fullest unfolding of the remarkable
   genius that created *A Raisin in the Sun*, and *Sidney Brustein's Window*.
   These plays are the lasting legacy of the extraordinarily gifted woman
   whom Julius Lester calls in his Foreword "the ultimate black writer for
   today . . . My God, how we need her."   (254140—$8.95)

☐ **FOUR PLAYS BY ARISTOPHANES, with translations by William Arrow-**
   smith, Richard Lattimore, and Douglass Parker. The acknowledged
   master of Greek comedy, Aristophanes brilliantly combines serious
   political satire with bawdiness, pyrotechnical bombast with delicate
   lyrics. Now this volume brings together his four most celebrated plays:
   The Clouds, *The Birds*, *Lysistrata*, and *The Frogs*. (007178—$5.95)

☐ **MA RAINEY'S BLACK BOTTOM, by August Wilson.** The time is is 1927.
   The place is a run-down recording studio in Chicago where Ma Rainey,
   the legendary blues singer is due to arrive. What goes down in the
   session to come is more than music, it is a riveting portrayal of black
   rage . . . of racism, of the self-hate that racism breeds, and of racial
   exploitation.   (256844—$5.95)

                Prices slightly higher in Canada.

            Buy them at your local bookstore or use this convenient
                        coupon for ordering.

NEW AMERICAN LIBRARY
P.O. Box 999, Bergenfield, New Jersey 07621

Please send me the books I have checked above. I am enclosing
$_____(please add $1.50 to this order to cover postage and
handling). Send check or money order—no cash or C.O.D.'s. Prices and
numbers are subject to change without notice.

Name_____

Address_____

City_____State_____Zip Code_____
                Allow 4-6 weeks for delivery.
        This offer is subject to withdrawal without notice.